Published by Modern Publishing
A Division of Unisystems, Inc.

Copyright © 1989 by Modern Publishing, a division of Unisystems, Inc.

TM – Pen Pals is a trademark of Modern Publishing,
a division of Unisystems, Inc.

®Honey Bear Books is a trademark owned by Honey Bear Productions, Inc.,
and is registered in the U.S. Patent and Trademark Office.

Printed in Belgium

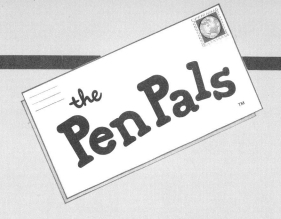

GRETA'S GRAND PRIZE

Written and Illustrated by Susan Marino

MODERN PUBLISHING
A Division of Unisystems, Inc.
New York, New York 10022

All of the essay contestants held their breath as the judge stepped up to announce the winner.

"The grand prize winner, for her essay, 'Friendship,' is Greta Goat!"

The audience applauded loudly. Happy and excited, Greta stepped forward to shake hands with the judge, and receive her prize.

"Greta," the judge said, "I'm pleased to announce you've won an all expense paid, week long trip for two to any place in the world!"

The audience applauded again, and Greta thanked the judge and waved at her mother, who would accompany her on her prize trip.

KERRY
KANGAROO

CHRIS
CROCODILE

BILLY
BUCK

PETEY
PANDA

PATSY
PENGUIN

LUCY
LLAMA

"Well, Greta," her mother said, "where shall we go?"

"I'd like to visit one of my pen pals," Greta said. "But which one?"
Greta was having trouble deciding between the six friends she had made
earlier that year in summer camp. The seven campers had made a pen pal
pact and had been writing to each other for months now.

Petey Panda had told Greta how wonderful China was, and she wanted to see the rice paddies and rickshaws he had described in his letters.

Chris Crocodile would show her the pyramids of Egypt.

Patsy Penguin would take her to see the icebergs of Antarctica, and they could watch the whales swimming by.

Billy Buck's forest home in the United States sounded like a wonderful place to visit.

So did Kerry Kangaroo's home in Australia. Kerry had told Greta his mother would take them both for a ride in her pouch if Greta ever came to visit.

And Lucy Llama had promised Greta a guided tour through the Andes Mountains if Greta ever visited her in Peru.

"I just can't choose between my friends," Greta told her mother. "I'm going to have to write a letter to the judge and return the grand prize."

Greta wrote a long letter explaining why she could not accept the prize and risk hurting her friends' feelings. "After all," she wrote, "I won the prize for my essay on friendship. I think it's more important that I be a good friend than that I accept the prize."

The contest judge read Greta's letter through twice, and then called a special meeting of the essay committee.

Two days later, Greta received a letter from the committee. They were so impressed with her letter that they decided to award her an even bigger prize: Instead of visiting one of her pen pals, *all of her pen pals were coming to visit her!*

And they had a wonderful time!

THE WORLD OF

Pacific
Ocean